This book should be returned to any branch of the
Lancashire County Library on or before the date shown

HOPSCOTCH
FAIRY TALES

Rapunzel

First published in 2008 by
Franklin Watts
338 Euston Road
London
NW1 3BH

Franklin Watts Australia
Level 17/207 Kent Street
Sydney
NSW 2000

A CIP catalogue record for this book is available
from the British Library.

ISBN 978 0 7496 7900 2 (hbk)
ISBN 978 0 7496 7906 4 (pbk)

Series Editor: Melanie Palmer
Series Advisor: Dr Barrie Wade
Series Designer: Peter Scoulding

Printed in China

Franklin Watts is a division of
Hachette Children's Books,
an Hachette Livre UK company.

'To Mary, my lovely sister, with love' P. K.

HOPSCOTCH
FAIRY TALES

Rapunzel

by Anne Walter and Peter Kavanagh

W
FRANKLIN WATTS
LONDON•SYDNEY

Once there lived a mean witch
who had a beautiful garden,
full of a plant called rapunzel.

6

Next door lived a poor husband and wife. The wife was going to have their first baby. She longed to eat the tasty rapunzel plants.

One day, the husband went to pick
some of the plants for his wife. Just
then, the mean witch jumped out.
"Those plants are mine!" she cried.

"They're for my wife," begged the husband. "She's having a baby." "Very well," said the witch. "You can live, but I will take your child."

The man rushed back to his wife.

She ate up all the rapunzel plants.

The man did not tell his wife about

the witch.

Soon, the wife had a baby girl.

At once, the witch appeared.

"The baby is mine!" she screamed.

"I'll call her Rapunzel, just like the plants you stole!" said the witch. She took the baby and left. The wife wept, but she could do nothing.

The witch locked Rapunzel in a tall tower with no door, surrounded by sharp thorns. Rapunzel grew into a beautiful girl with long, golden hair.

As time passed, Rapunzel's hair grew longer. The witch often went to see her in the tower.

"Rapunzel, Rapunzel, let down your hair," she shouted up.

14

Whenever Rapunzel heard the witch, she untied her hair and let it fall down to the ground. Up and up the witch climbed.

15

Rapunzel was always lonely. She sang to keep herself company. One day, a prince was riding by. He stopped as he heard her sweet voice.

He looked up and
saw the beautiful girl
in the tower. He saw
how the witch climbed
up her long, golden hair.

The prince waited until the witch left. "Rapunzel, Rapunzel, let down your hair!" he called. She let it down and he climbed up.

Instead of an ugly witch, Rapunzel saw the handsome prince! They fell in love straight away and the prince asked her to marry him.

Rapunzel longed to be the prince's wife, but she was trapped.

"How can I leave this tower?" she asked. "There's no way out!"

"Take this silk," said the prince.
"I will bring some every day.
Tie the pieces together until they
reach the ground. Then you can
climb down!"

As the prince rushed away, the witch saw him. She was furious. She called to Rapunzel and quickly raced up the tower.

"You have betrayed me!" the witch screamed. She cut off all Rapunzel's hair, and banished her to the woods.

The witch waited and waited.

At last, she heard the prince shout:

"Rapunzel, Rapunzel, let down

your hair."

The witch hid behind the wall and lowered the locks of hair down to the prince.

The prince climbed up, but when
he got to the top he saw ...
the angry witch!

He was so shocked, he let go of
the hair and fell down, landing
on the sharp thorns below.

The thorns cut the prince's eyes. He could not see. He crawled through the woods for days until he heard a sweet voice singing.

He stumbled towards the voice.
Just then Rapunzel opened her
cottage door and saw him.

"My poor prince!" she cried.

Rapunzel's tears fell on the prince's face. They soothed his scratched eyes and he could see again!

Rapunzel and the prince were never parted again. They lived happily ever after.

Hopscotch has been specially designed to fit the requirements of the Literacy Framework. It offers real books by top authors and illustrators for children developing their reading skills. There are 55 Hopscotch stories to choose from:

* hardback